THE MERRY PRANKS OF TILL EULENSPIEGEL

Adapted by Heinz Janisch
Illustrated by Lisbeth Zwerger
Translated by Anthea Bell

A Michael Neugebauer Book
NORTH-SOUTH BOOKS/NEW YORK/LONDON

TILL'S THREE BAPTISMS

If you want to be a famous practical joker like Till Eulenspiegel and get away with it, then you must learn to keep your head above water.

Till Eulenspiegel learned young. When he was a little baby, howling and bawling, Till was taken to church like any other child to be baptized.

There stood the worthy priest, waiting to baptize little Till with holy water in the Lord's name, as is right and proper.

So Till had his first baptism with holy water, to the glory of God and His saints, and there was no harm in that.

But on the way home, when the christening party had been eating and drinking and dancing and making merry, well, on the way home the woman carrying Till happened to fall full-length and *splash!*—there lay little Till in the dusty, dirty road, right in the middle of a puddle.

So Till was baptized a second time—with the dirty water of the high road, in which wandering folk and vagabonds are baptized.

No sooner was the christening party home than little Till went straight into a tub of water.

And there he sat, tiny and naked, laughing merrily, while his mother scrubbed him and scoured him until he looked as good as new.

So Till was baptized a third time, in hot water, and he was to feel at home getting into hot water for the rest of his life.

And that's how Till Eulenspiegel had three baptisms and learned to keep his head above water.

TILL IN THE   BEEHIVE

Who would want to miss a feast or a fair, where there's music for dancing, paper roses, and cotton candy? That's what young Till thought, and off he went happily to the village fair, where he laughed and sang and drank, until he was so weary he could hardly keep on his feet.

I'll find a good place to rest, thought Till. When he saw several large, empty wicker beehives like baskets standing in a farmyard, he got into one, closed the lid, and started snoring so loudly, you might have thought there were a thousand bees buzzing inside.

That night, along came two thieves to steal a beehive. They took the one with Till inside it and secretly carried it away through the dark. When the swaying of the hive woke Till, he heard the two men talking about the beehive they had stolen, and money, and the long way they had to go. Cautiously, he raised the lid of the wicker hive, put out his hand, and pulled the hair of the thief who was walking in front.

"Hey there," called the thief to his friend, "are you crazy? Why are you pulling my hair like that?"

"I never pulled your hair!" said the man at the back, surprised. "I haven't a hand free! I'm carrying this hive, so how could I pull your hair?"

Not long afterward, Till pulled the hair of the man walking at the back so hard that he let out a yell of rage and accused the man in front of hurting him. And so it went on for quite a while longer, this way and that, until at last they came to blows and had a great fight, chasing one another. They put the basket down, and then they ran and they ran.

Till closed the lid of the basket hive again, and he slept until the sun shone through the wickerwork.

Then he lifted the lid of the beehive, blinking at the bright light. The morning sun had warmed the beehive. Till sat there a while longer, enjoying the comfort of it.

But his head was still humming with all the wine he had drunk at the fair, humming and buzzing like, well, like a beehive.

TILL ON THE TIGHTROPE

Some folks will pick up a pair of scissors and know they're cut out to be tailors.

Others will draw a straight line and know they're designed to be architects.

But as for young Till Eulenspiegel, he stretched a rope across the rooftops, and at once he knew: I'm a flighty fellow and I always will be. I'm going to tread a tightrope all my life!

One day Till's mother, who would much rather he had been an architect or a tailor, took the scissors he despised and cut the rope just as he was walking it.

How folks laughed to see the bold, high-flying Till stumble in midair, tumble off the rope, and fall on his nose!

But the very next morning Till was back up there on his rope again. And he called down to all the folks standing below and looking up at him, "Give me all your left shoes! Tie them to a long rope, and I'll show you a clever trick!"

Well, most of them did as Till said, and then they had to reel about on one leg, hopping up and down like sick birds. Some of them leaned against each other, back to back, to keep their balance.

"Here I stand, steady as a rock, on my thin rope," Till called down, seeing the people hop about, "and there you go, reeling and swaying and staggering like that, as if you didn't have firm ground underfoot at all!"

Whereupon he took a pair of scissors out of his coat pocket and cut the rope with the shoes tied to it in half—right above the heads of all those folks.

Shoes large and small, shoes broad and narrow, shoes heavy and light fell on their heads—boots and sandals, silken slippers, wooden clogs and all rained down.

"There are your shoes back!" called Till.

He settled comfortably on his rope and watched them all begin scuffling for their shoes.

Well, thought Till, rocking happily on his rope high above the rooftops, see how easy it is to catch you folks off balance!

TILL WOULD LIKE TO FLY

If a man were to lean too far out of a high upstairs window or jump off a roof, well, he'd fall like a stone and break every bone in his body. Everyone knows that.

So you can imagine what a stir it made when Till came to a town one day and let it be known he was planning to fly.

"I'd like to fly off the tower of the town hall," Till told the mayor and the people of the town.

So crowds of people gathered in the square outside the town hall, and Till climbed the tower.

He climbed on the roof and made ready. He took a deep breath, and he flapped his arms as best he could. Some people expected to see him take off any minute and fly across the square.

Then Till stopped flapping his arms. He straightened up, and he called down to the folks below, "You may think I'm birdbrained, you may think I'm cuckoo, but that doesn't mean I can fly. I said I'd like to fly, and so I would. Wouldn't we all? But the fact is, as you saw for yourselves, I'm afraid I can't!"

Then he calmly climbed down from the tower and walked away.

Some of the people grumbled angrily, but most of them laughed and said, "He's right, to be sure! He only said he'd like to fly. And after all, how could he?"

"He's such a joker, though," grumbled one old man, thoughtfully. "I reckoned a joker like Till Eulenspiegel could fly. You just don't know whom to trust nowadays!"

"Oh, look!" cried a little girl. "There he flies!"

Everyone stopped and looked up at the sky.

"Where, where?" shouted the old man in excitement.

But the little girl was only joking herself, and she laughed and ran away as fast as she could go.

"There, you see?" said one of the women to the old man. "We're still ready to believe anything!"

TILL BAKES OWLS AND MONKEYS

"What a crazy fellow!" folks say when they hear of Till's merry pranks. And a few of the clever sort, who haven't forgotten how to laugh, will add, "And thank goodness there are people like Till around—folks who will do any crazy thing they please—or what a dull world it would be!"

Well, one day Till came to the shop of a baker who urgently needed an assistant. After he had worked there a few days, the master baker asked Till to do the baking that night and said it must all be done by morning.

"What am I to bake, then?" asked Till.

The master baker lost his temper. "What do you think, in a baker's shop?" he said sarcastically. "Owls and monkeys, to be sure!"

So, early in the morning, when the baker came down, he found not a single ordinary loaf or roll in his bakery. The dough had all been baked into the shapes of owls and monkeys. Owls and monkeys of all sizes, everywhere he looked.

"Are you out of your mind?" asked the furious master baker. "What on earth have you been baking?"

"What you told me to bake," said Till calmly. "Owls and monkeys."

The baker swore, and was very angry, and would not calm down. "Take your stupid owls and monkeys and get out!" he shouted, red in the face.

And he made Till pay for the dough he had wasted. So Till gave the baker the money, put all his owls and monkeys in a basket, and went on his way.

He stood outside the church and showed the owls and monkeys he had baked to everyone who came by, young and old, and the children, too. And as it was St. Nicholas's Eve, and all the people were looking for little presents to give each other, Till's owls and monkeys were just what they wanted.

"Something new at last," said they. "A nice change from those boring old round rolls!"

And they bought and bought, and so Till earned much more money than he had given the baker for the dough.

TILL BUYS LAND

One man may own many acres of land where great, dark forests of thousands of trees grow, while another has just three silver birches in his garden, and a third has nothing but a tiny plant in a flowerpot. Whose land would you say was worth most to him?

Having only a tiny bit of land of your own may save your life, as Till found out on his travels.

He happened to be passing through a country whose king had forbidden him ever to set foot in it again, on pain of death.

Now all of a sudden Till heard the king and his court coming near.

In great haste, he went up to a farmer who was plowing his field.

"Is this your land?" Till asked.

"That it is. I inherited it," said the farmer in surprise. "Yes, the land is mine."

"Will you sell me just enough earth to fill my little cart here?" Till asked him.

Well, the farmer agreed. Till shoveled earth into the cart as fast as he could, and then got in.

So when the king came by, he saw Till Eulenspiegel sitting in the cart, buried up to his neck in earth.

"What are you doing here?" asked the angry king. "Didn't I forbid you ever to set foot in my land again?"

"Oh, but I'm not in your land, my lord king," said Till. "This is my own land. I bought it just now, from that farmer. All you see in this cart belongs to me."

At that the king had to laugh, and he let Till off again one more time.

Till mounted his horse and rode fast away. But he left the cart full of earth behind, and there it stands to this day.

All it contains, to be sure, is Till's little bit of earthbound land—for his real land is the land of merry pranks, and anyone who wants to visit that land is welcome!

TILL AND THE DONKEY

Till never had much time for scholars and professors and learned folk. He would play a trick on them whenever he could.

One day he put up a notice saying he was a very clever fellow who could teach any fool to read in no time at all.

So some of the learned men who heard of it thought of a mean trick to play on Till, and they brought him an old donkey. Surely, they told Till, he could teach that donkey to read! Why, it would be child's play to such a clever man!

"There are plenty of donkeys, both young and old, among folks who can read already," said Till, and he bowed low and took the donkey away with him.

He led the donkey to the nearest stable, took out an old prayer book, and put it in the manger. Then he sprinkled some oats between the pages of the book. Soon the hungry donkey was eagerly leafing through it with his nose to get at the oats. When he came to a place in the book where there weren't any oats, he brayed aloud, "Hee-haw!"

Till went to the learned men and asked them to come the next day and see for themselves what he had taught the donkey. And he gave the donkey no more to eat after that, so that he would be hungry for his oats.

Next morning the learned men came along with several students. Full of curiosity, they gathered around Till and his donkey.

Till fetched out his book, and put it in front of the donkey's nose. And the donkey began leafing through it with his nose, but he found no oats.

He began braying, at the top of his voice, "Hee-haw! Hee-haw!"

"You see," said Till proudly, "I've already taught him two words. He can read 'he' and 'or,' and he'll be able to read all the rest pretty soon."

The learned men were very angry, and they went away. Till had fooled them yet again.

It would take more time than I can spare to educate all these donkeys, thought Till, as he went cheerfully on his way.

TILL'S UPHILL JOURNEY

Walking does you good, say people who like to walk, and they go on long journeys on foot, up hill and down dale, and through many lands.

Well, once Till was on his travels along with a group of pilgrims. They were on their way to Rome, to see the pope and the famous cathedral of St. Peter's.

As they were crossing the Alps, a strange thing happened. Whenever the path led steeply uphill, and they were all puffing and panting and making their weary way forward, step by step, Till would run up the slope, singing and laughing, as if he could wish for nothing better.

But when the road led downhill, and they were all hurrying down, light of foot, relaxing after the uphill climb, Till grumbled and stumbled crossly after them, looking as if it were pain and grief to him.

"Master Till, I don't understand you a bit," said one of the pilgrims at last. "Going uphill, the difficult part, you're merry and in a good temper, but going downhill, the easy part, you moan and groan. What does it mean?"

"Easy!" said Till. "When I'm going uphill, I'm looking forward to the wonderful view from the top and the bit of rest I'll take. And from up there I'll be able see if that was the last mountain on our way, or if there's another to come. But when I'm going downhill, all I can see is the deep valley into which I must go and the next mountain ahead of me. Why would I be glad of that?"

They went on their way for many more days and weeks.
Till stumbled unhappily downhill and ran merrily uphill.
Not until he was at the top of the last hill and saw
the city of Rome lying ahead of him did he run
merrily down the hillside, too.

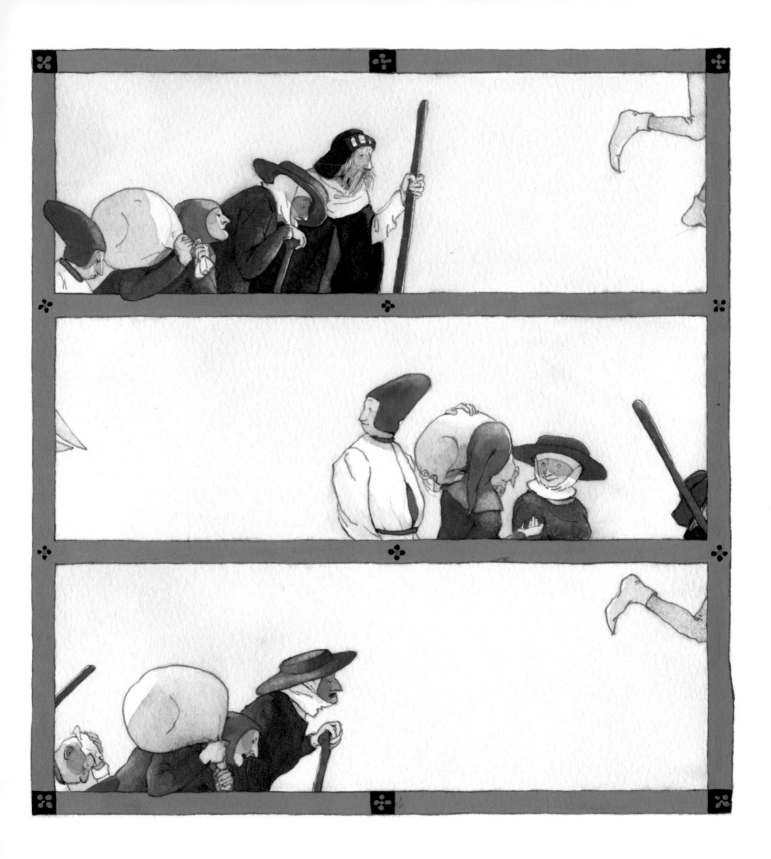

TILL COMES TO THE SEA

Till liked to travel. He went from village to village, across country, over fields and meadows, over mountains and hills, just as he liked. The long way round is a good way to go, he often said, and then he would set off, following his nose.

So one day Till came to the sea.

There he stood, on the shore, drinking in the sight of its mighty blue expanse.

He was strolling slowly along the beach when he saw some men swimming in the water. All of a sudden they began to shout in great alarm.

"One of us must have drowned!" cried one of the men. "There were nine of us when we went into the water, and now there are only eight!"

So they all counted the others, and they all made it eight. But none of them had counted himself. Every single one of them forgot that he was the ninth.

Sad and gloomy, they swam ashore.

"Why are you so sad?" asked Till, who had been watching them.

"There were nine of us when we came here, and now there are only eight. One of us must have drowned!" wailed the men.

"Well, there's only one way to find out for sure," said Till. "Lie down on the ground, all of you, and bury your noses in the sand as deep as you can!"

The men lay down and buried their noses in the sand.

"There—now stand up and count the holes your noses have left," Till told them.

The men counted, and one of them cried in surprise, "Why, there are nine holes!"

"That's an easy sum," said Till. "Nine holes—nine noses. Nine noses—nine men!"

"Nine noses—nine men!" cried the friends, and laughing, they flung their arms around each other.

They hugged and kissed Till, too, and made a great fuss over him.

"If you're ever in trouble again," said Till, "then hold on to your own noses. You can always rely on your nose!"

And he said good-bye and strolled slowly away, still following his nose.

TILL MAKES GREEN INTO BLUE

Some folks will believe anything. If you're clever enough you can get them to believe green is blue.

Till did just that one day when he was at market and saw a farmer buying some good green cloth. It was nearly winter, and Till was freezing cold.

He found two of his friends and told them his plan.

Well, when the farmer was strolling out of town, carrying his good green cloth, Till came up to him and said, "Excuse me, master, but where did you get that good blue cloth?"

"This cloth is green, friend," said the farmer in surprise.

So Till beckoned to one of his friends, who was pretending to be an ordinary strolling fellow passing by.

"Excuse me, sir," said Till to him, "but we can't agree about the color of this good cloth here. Tell us yourself—is it green, or is it blue?"

"What a question!" said the man. "Blue, of course. How can you doubt it?"

Now the farmer began to feel less sure of himself.

"Here comes a monk," said Till. "Let's ask him, too."

But the monk was Till's second friend, and he was in the plot as well.

"If he says this cloth is blue as well," said the farmer, "then it's yours. For I'd sooner believe a churchman than two wandering vagabonds."

So they asked the monk, and the monk, too, said, "What a fine blue cloth that is! You made a good purchase there!"

"If you say so as well," cried the poor farmer, "then I suppose it must be right. Here, take this blue cloth. I want nothing more to do with it!"

So Till and his two friends got that good green cloth for nothing.

And while the gullible farmer had to freeze in his torn old coat, the three of them went to the tailor and had warm clothes made for the winter.

TILL'S LAST PRANK

Many a tale is told of Till Eulenspiegel's death, but no one knows for certain how it was. Some say they buried him the wrong way up, face downward.

Others say the rope broke as the coffin was being let down, and now he stands upright in his grave.

And argue as folk may about the way Till lay in his grave—the wrong way up, or standing upright, in as comical a manner as he lived—there was plenty of argument about his last will and testament, too, when it was made known.

Till had divided all he had into three parts: one part for his friends, one part for the town councillors, and one part for the priest.

It was all kept in a great chest, which wasn't to be opened until Till was buried.

After the funeral, his friends and the town councillors and the priest all met to open the chest together.

They were expecting money, and precious jewels, for they knew of Till Eulenspiegel's journeys through many lands.

But when they opened the heavy lid of the chest, they found nothing but ordinary stones—plain, grey stones—inside it. Till's friends accused the town councillors of stealing all the money away in secret and putting stones inside the chest instead.

The town councillors were convinced that Till's friends had taken it all away the night before.

And the priest felt sure he had been cheated by Till's friends and the town councillors and thought they meant to play a trick on him.

Before long there was a fierce quarrel going on. They were talking at the tops of their voices, and arguing, and fighting. They could be heard shouting angrily until the early hours of the morning.

So Till had one final prank up his sleeve to play as he made his escape
for the very last time.

First published in the United States in 1990 by Picture Book Studio.
Reissued in the United States, Great Britain, Canada, Australia, and
New Zealand in 2000 by North-South Books, an imprint of
Nord-Süd Verlag AG, Gossau Zürich, Switzerland.
Copyright © 1990 by Nord-Süd Verlag AG, Gossau Zürich, Switzerland
First published in Switzerland under the title Till Eulenspiegel
English translation copyright © 1990 by North-South Books Inc.
All rights reserved. No part of this book may be reproduced or utilized in any form
or by any means, electronic or mechanical, including photocopying,
recording, or any information storage and retrieval system,
without permission in writing from the publisher.
Distributed in the United States by North-South Books Inc., New York.
Library of Congress Cataloging in Publication Data
[Till Eulenspiegel, English]
The merry pranks of Till Eulenspiegel/from a retelling by Heinz Janisch;
illustrated by Lisbeth Zwerger; translated by Anthea Bell.
Translation of: Till Eulenspiegel.
Summary: Unfolds the life of the merry prankster Till, from his rowdy infancy
to his final joke at his own funeral.
[1. Folklore—Germany.] I. Zwerger, Lisbeth, ill. II. Bell, Anthea. III. Title.
PZ8.1.J33Me 1990
398.22'0943—dc20
[E]   90-7168
A CIP catalogue record for this book is available from The British Library.
ISBN 1-55858-806-X (trade binding) 10 9 8 7 6 5 4 3 2 1
Printed in Italy
For more information about our books, and the authors and artists
who create them, visit our web site: www.northsouth.com

Other North-South books illustrated by Lisbeth Zwerger:
ALICE IN WONDERLAND by Lewis Carroll
THE CANTERVILLE GHOST by Oscar Wilde
THE DELIVERERS OF THEIR COUNTRY by E. Nesbit
DWARF NOSE by Wilhelm Hauff
THE LEGEND OF ROSEPETAL by Clemens Brentano
LITTLE HOBBIN by Theodor Storm
LITTLE RED CAP by Jacob and Wilhelm Grimm
LULLABIES, LYRICS AND GALLOWS SONGS by Christian Morgenstern
THE NIGHTINGALE by Hans Christian Andersen
NOAH'S ARK retold by Heinz Janisch
THE SWINEHERD by Hans Christian Andersen
THE WIZARD OF OZ by L. Frank Baum
THE ART OF LISBETH ZWERGER